P9-DNI-189

MOTHER LUCY GOOSEY

CINDERFELLA

ROSIE RINGAROUNDA

PINA BUTTAH-GELEÉ

ELLA MENOPIPI

The HIPS on the DRAG QUEEN Go Swish, Swish, Swish

by

Lil Miss Hot Mess

Illustrated by

Olga de Dios

RP | KIDS
PHILADELPHIA

Copyright © 2020 by Lil Miss Hot Mess
Illustrations copyright © 2020 by Olga de Dios
Cover copyright © 2020 by Hachette Book Group, Inc.

Hachette Book Group supports the right to free expression and the value of copyright.
The purpose of copyright is to encourage writers and artists to produce
the creative works that enrich our culture.

The scanning, uploading, and distribution of this book without permission
is a theft of the author's intellectual property. If you would like permission to use
material from the book (other than for review purposes), please contact
permissions@hbgusa.com. Thank you for your support of the author's rights.

Running Press Kids
Hachette Book Group
1290 Avenue of the Americas, New York, NY 10104
www.runningpress.com/rpkids
@RP_Kids

Printed in China

First Edition: May 2020

Published by Running Press Kids, an imprint of Perseus Books, LLC,
a subsidiary of Hachette Book Group, Inc. The Running Press Kids name and
logo is a trademark of the Hachette Book Group.

The Hachette Speakers Bureau provides a wide range of authors for speaking events.
To find out more, go to www.hachettespeakersbureau.com or call (866) 376-6591.

The publisher is not responsible for websites (or their content)
that are not owned by the publisher.

Print book cover and interior design by Frances J. Soo Ping Chow.

Library of Congress Control Number: 2019937979

ISBNs: 978-0-7624-6765-5 (hardcover), 978-0-7624-6764-8 (ebook)

APS

10 9 8 7 6 5 4 3

For Lily and Edith, and all the future
queens-in-training at Camp Hot Mess.

—LMHM

May these illustrations motivate us
to color our lives with fantasy and freedom.

—OdD

The hips on the drag queen go
SWISH, SWISH, SWISH.

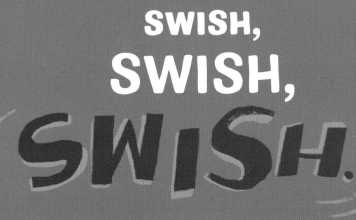

SWISH,
SWISH,
SWISH.

SWISH,
SWISH,
SWISH.

The hips on the drag queen go
SWISH, SWISH, SWISH...

ALL THROUGH THE TOWN!

The hair on the drag queen goes
UP, UP, UP.

The hair on the drag queen goes **UP, UP, UP...**

ALL THROUGH THE TOWN!

The shoes on the drag queen go
STOMP, STOMP, STOMP.

STOMP,
STOMP,
STOMP.
STOMP,
STOMP,
STOMP

The shoes on the drag queen go
STOMP, STOMP, STOMP...

ALL THROUGH THE TOWN!

The jewels on the drag queen go
BLING, BLING, BLING.

BLING,
BLING,

BLING.

BLING, ◆ BLING,
BLING.

The jewels on the drag queen go **BLING, BLING, BLING...**

ALL THROUGH THE TOWN!

The shoulders on the drag queen go
SHIMMY, SHIMMY, SHIMMY.

SHIMMY,
SHIMMY,
SHIMMY.

SHIMMY,
SHIMMY,
SHIMMY.

The shoulders on the drag queen go
SHIMMY, SHIMMY, SHIMMY...

ALL THROUGH THE TOWN!

The cheeks on the drag queen go
BLUSH, BLUSH, BLUSH.

BLUSH,

BLUSH,

BLUSH.

BLUSH,

BLUSH,

BLUSH.

The cheeks on the drag queen go
BLUSH, BLUSH, BLUSH...

ALL THROUGH THE TOWN!

The fingers on the drag queen go
SNAP, SNAP, SNAP.

SNAP,
SNAP,
SNAP.

SNAP,
SNAP,
SNAP.

The fingers on the drag queen go
SNAP, SNAP, SNAP...

ALL THROUGH THE TOWN!

The mouth on the drag queen goes
BLAH, BLAH, BLAH.

BLAH, BLAH, BLAH.

BLAH, BLAH, BLAH.

The mouth on
the drag queen goes
BLAH, BLAH, BLAH...

ALL THROUGH THE TOWN!

The dance of the drag queen goes
TWIRL, TWIRL, TWIRL.

TWIRL,
TWIRL,
TWIRL.

TWIRL,
TWIRL,
TWIRL.

The dance of the drag queen goes
TWIRL, TWIRL, TWIRL...

ALL THROUGH THE TOWN!

FRIDA BEA MEE

JACLYN JILL

STINKERBELLE

RITA BOOKE